PIA AND THE TREE OF WISDOM

EXCITING AND INSPIRATIONAL STORIES FOR GIRLS ABOUT SELF-AWARENESS, INNER-STRENGTH AND COURAGE

KATE BURNELL

ISBN - 9798728820895

THIS BOOK BELONGS TO

_____

CONTENTS

INTRODUCTION

Welcome to the delightful world of Pia, a courageous and high-spirited young girl who always has people's best interest at heart and strives to make them happy. You might be wondering what's so special about this one little girl. Well, in Pia's world, she experiences fantastical encounters which cannot always be explained, but which help her and her new friends grow to understand how the world works and how it can become a better place. In this collection of short stories, we get to discover the true spirit of bravery, truth, strength, self-confidence and love as we delve into little Pia's world. A world in which she gets to question all that she knows about what it means to grow up.

I hope you enjoy these stories as much as I enjoyed writing them. Now, sit back and get ready to meet your new friends as we enter Pia's world.

STORY 1 – PIA AND THE TREE OF WISDOM

Pia stood at the kitchen window, looking out at a garden that stretched on for what felt like miles and miles ahead.

"Is this really all ours?" she asked her mother who stood beside her.

Pia's mother had splatters of blue paint on her face and overalls, and she held a paint brush which she pointed as she spoke.

"All the way down to that low, long hedge at the end of the field."

Pia had never seen so much green space before. She had just moved to the village of Heely with her parents and everything was so new and different. Especially as they had come from an enormous city where all the buildings stretched sky high and the gardens were little green boxes in the middle of a sea of concrete.

"And do I get to play out there?" Pia asked, unsure of what to do with such expanse.

Her mother smiled as she replied, "The best place for an eight-year-old to play is outside in fresh air."

Pia was excited about this and couldn't wait to go outside, but she was also a little bit concerned. Because right by the hedge at the end of the garden, there stood a big old, scary looking oak tree.

Even from that distance, Pia could tell it was an odd one, with crooked, drooping branches and a twisted, dark trunk as wide as a car. Small green leaves hung from its branches like little hands, swaying gently with the wind. Pia was certain she would not be going anywhere near the creepy oak tree.

All day long, Pia stayed in the house and helped her mother as they painted the walls of their new home in mixed colours of blue, teal and white, which just happened to be Pia's favourite colours. They were finishing just in time to have tea when her father came back home, holding a small grey carrier case.

Pia's eyes widened with surprise when she saw what was inside.

"A puppy!" she squealed.

Her father opened the small door and a little dog jumped out. Its fur was patchy brown and white, and it had big, black eyes, with a pink tongue which hung out as it tried to lick Pia's smiling face.

"We thought you might be lonely after moving away from your friends," Pia's father said. "I'm sure you'll make new pals once school starts in the autumn, but this little guy will keep you company."

Pia was really grateful and thanked them both with big, warm hugs.

"I think we should call him Dusty," she suggested, "because he looks like he's covered in specks of dust."

Dusty barked and wagged his tail, and they all took that as a sign of approval. With Dusty by her side, Pia was not so afraid of exploring the large garden on her own.

"Remember not to go past the hedge at the end of the garden," her mother cautioned Pia the next day when she put on her shoes to go outside. "There's a busy road on the other side and we don't want you or Dusty to get hurt."

But Pia had no plans of ever going that far, not when the big, old tree was still out there.

With Dusty by her side, Pia raced around the grassy field and spent all morning chasing after bright coloured butterflies and bushytailed grey squirrels. She had never had so much fun doing almost nothing at all.

Every day that week, Pia remembered her mother's words and made sure not to stray near the hedge. But as time went by, Dusty became bolder, and he would run closer and closer to the oak tree each day. He was still only a puppy and wouldn't always listen when Pia asked him to stop.

One day, as Pia tried to teach Dusty how to fetch a ball, she tossed it gently like she always did, but the grass was still wet from the morning's rain and the ball rolled right towards the scary oak tree. Dusty barked excitedly and ran with speed to fetch the ball.

Pia watched in dismay as the ball kept rolling past the tree. It carried on straight for the hedge at the end of the garden until it disappeared into a small gap she hadn't noticed before.

To make matters worse, the puppy didn't stop running. He ran so fast that his red collar got caught against one of the bushes in the hedge.

"Oh no!" Pia cried.

Dusty's bark was filled with panic this time. The more he struggled, the more his collar twisted within the bushes. And the more he moved to free himself, the closer he got to breaking out to the busy road on the other side.

Even though she knew she had to save him, Pia was frozen in fear. To get to Dusty, she would have to go past the tree's sagging branches which looked like they were waiting to reach down and swoop her right up.

"Go on! What are you waiting for?" a soft fluttery voice called out.

At first, Pia wasn't sure if she had heard correctly. She looked from side to side.

"Who said that?" she asked, for there was no one around.

"Don't be afraid, there's no one else here but me," the voice said.

The only person out there was Pia. It was then that she realised the voice had come from the tree.

"B-b-but you're an old oak tree," she stuttered in disbelief.

The small green leaves rustled lightly, as if the tree was laughing. "I am not just any old tree. I am the Tree of Wisdom, one of the Great Whispering Oaks of Heely."

Pia still couldn't believe her ears. The voice was clearly coming from the tree, but there had to be someone hiding behind it. She was too frightened to walk around and catch whoever was playing this trick on her.

Just then, there was a whimpering sound from the hedge. In her shock, Pia had almost forgotten about Dusty.

"You have to hurry or the puppy will hurt himself," the tree urged. "I know you're afraid, but sometimes in life, we need to push through our fears to do the right thing. If we work together, we can set him free quickly."

Pia was still frightened, but she knew the tree was right. So she took a deep breath and ran past the tree's trunk and towards the hedge. She was relieved when no branches reached down to grab her.

Dusty had worked himself even further into the small gap.

"You will have to help him unwind his collar from the bushes," the tree said.

Pia did as it said, making sure to hold Dusty still. She could hear the cars and trucks on the other side of the hedge. Her mother's words were on her mind, it would be dangerous if they crossed over.

Twisting and turning, she worked the collar free and breathed a sigh of relief when Dusty barked and licked her face. The puppy was so happy to be free, he ran back into the field, chasing a yellow-winged butterfly and yapping with delight.

"Thanks for helping me save Dusty," Pia said to the tree, even though she was still a little scared. She would never have imagined that trees could speak, or that one would help her save Dusty.

"Thank you for listening to me," the tree replied, its leaves swaying with the sound. "It was also your bravery that helped save your puppy. You overcame your fears and went ahead to help him when he was in need."

Pia was intrigued. And now she wasn't too scared to walk around the tree to check if all this was a cruel trick.

"You must be very old to be so big," she said, as she walked around its wide trunk.

"I took root here many hundreds of years ago. Long before that house was built, and even before the road was formed. That is very old, indeed."

Pia had found no one behind the tree. She stopped and looked up at the long branches. There was nobody up there either.

"Are you called the Tree of Wisdom because you're so old?" she asked.

The tree chuckled. "Not everyone older is wiser, young girl. We must always listen and decide for yourselves if the advice we are given is worth acting upon. It has been so long since anyone who came down here was willing to free their senses and hear my voice."

At that moment, Pia's mother called her name from the house.

"I hope you'll come back and visit me soon," the tree said. "It's lonely out here at the end of the field with nothing but cars and trucks speeding by."

Pia ran all the way back to the house and nearly knocked her mother over in her excitement.

"Mummy, the oak tree helped me save Dusty from the hedge."

"The oak tree?" her mother laughed as she replied. "I'm sure you just heard the wind out there."

Pia was about to insist that she was certain of what she had heard, when she remembered what the tree had said. Only those who were willing to free their senses could hear it speak. She looked out of the window and saw that the tree looked just like any other tree. Why would her mother believe her?

Suddenly, one of its branches shook and the leaves shimmered in the sunlight, as if the tree was waving at her.

Pia smiled and waved back at it, knowing she would go back tomorrow to visit the Tree of Wisdom.

STORY 2 – PIA AND THE TRUTH PROBLEM

One day, whilst Pia was reading her favourite book on the sofa in the living room, there was a loud knock at the front door. When her father answered it, she heard a stranger speaking to him. They had not received many visitors since they moved to Heely, so she was curious to see who this was.

"My name is Mrs Marble. I just wanted to welcome you to the village," a woman's voice said, "and to introduce my son. I'm sure your daughter will be happy to make a new friend."

Pia jumped up from the sofa eagerly. Even though Dusty was a lot of fun to be with, she really missed playing with other children. She ran out to the hallway and saw a tall woman standing outside with a boy with sandy coloured hair who looked about Pia's age. They both had big, bright smiles on their faces.

"This is Tommy," the woman introduced her son to Pia. "You two will be in the same class when school starts in the autumn."

Pia couldn't wait to tell Tommy all about the Tree of Wisdom. So far, neither her mother nor father had ventured anywhere near the big oak tree.

When Tommy's mother came in to have some tea with Pia's mother and father, Pia took Tommy into the garden to play with Dusty.

"Do you believe in magic?" she whispered to Tommy when they were alone.

Tommy gave her a funny look and shook his head. "There's no such thing as magic," he said with a sneer.

"I used to think so too, until I met the Tree of Wisdom. If you come with me to the end of the garden, I'll introduce you to the tree."

"That's just silly talk," Tommy laughed. "I'd rather play with Dusty here."

"The tree is truly magical!" Pia insisted. "If you follow me, you'll see for yourself."

But Tommy shook his head and wouldn't budge. "If you're going to tell lies, I don't want to be friends with you," he declared.

Pia's eyes filled with tears at being called a liar. Tommy wouldn't even go with her to the tree, so how could she prove her words were true? With no way to convince him, Pia stayed near the house with Tommy and Dusty instead, but she was very upset.

Not long after, it began to drizzle and the kids had to go back inside.

"Why don't you come to ours in a few days," Mrs Marble invited them over for lunch as they left.

Pia's parents were keen, but Pia couldn't bring herself to smile.

"Didn't you have a good time today?" her mother asked once their guests were gone. She could see Pia looked down.

Pia knew her mother had never heard the oak tree speak, so she wouldn't understand if she told her what happened.

"What would you do if someone doesn't believe something you said, even though it is true?"

Her mother guessed this person might be Tommy, but she didn't pry. Instead, she gave Pia a hug and told her what she would do if she was in her shoes.

"I would try my best to prove to the person that I am telling the truth, but you also have to decide if it is worth the effort if they don't give you a chance to do so."

The only way Pia could convince Tommy that she wasn't lying was by getting him to meet the tree, and so she thought hard that night about exactly how she would do this. The next day, still with no plan in hand, Pia went down to the tree and asked for its help.

"It never feels good to be called untruthful," the tree's musical voice came through its leaves once again, "especially if it is a misunderstanding. But I have an idea of how you can get him to see your way."

After the tree whispered its plan to Pia, she nodded because she thought it was a good one.

That weekend, Pia and her parents went for lunch at Tommy's house. Tommy was happy to see her and took her outside to play.

"My dad helped me build a fort with some logs not far from the river. It's very small, but we can both fit in it and watch the otters who swim in the water."

This sounded like a great idea to Pia, and she was looking forward to seeing an otter for the very first time. But she remembered the Tree of Wisdom's idea and crossed her hands in dismissal.

"Otters? That's just silly talk, there are no otters around here," she said with a frown.

Tommy stared at her in disbelief. "But I'm not lying," he assured her, "I've seen them once or twice already."

Pia shook her head. "I'd rather stay here and play with things I know are real."

Now, Tommy looked really glum and he didn't know what else to say to her. To Pia's dismay, it looked like he was about to cry, and that had not been her intention at all.

"I didn't mean to upset you, Tommy. I just thought you should see how it feels when you tell the truth and the other person doesn't give you a chance to prove it."

When Tommy realised what she meant, his mood lifted immediately. "I'm really sorry if I hurt your feelings, Pia. I didn't realise my words would be so hurtful. I promise I'll go see this tree when next we come to visit you."

Pia was relieved the plan had worked, and now she could follow Tommy to his fort. It was a small shed built from round logs stacked on top of each other. And it wasn't too close to the riverbed, so Pia wasn't worried about falling into the water.

They spent the hour looking out for otters until Tommy's mother called them in for lunch. Even though they didn't see any otters that day, Pia was certain she would spot them another time because she believed Tommy had been telling the truth.

The next weekend, Tommy came over to play and Pia took him straight to the end of the garden where the oak tree stood. She really hoped he would be willing to free his senses so he could hear the tree when it spoke.

"I'd like you to meet the Tree of Wisdom," Pia announced when they were under its dark, spidery branches, "one of the Great Whispering Oaks of Heely."

Tommy looked up at the odd-looking tree with an uncertain stare.

"Do I just talk to it?" he asked.

"You could start with introducing yourself," the tree said, and Tommy jumped back in fright.

Pia couldn't help smiling to herself. She was glad he could also hear the voice.

"My name is Tommy," Tommy stammered as he walked around the tree to check where the voice was coming from, just as Pia had done. "I'm sorry I didn't believe you were real before."

"We can sometimes miss out on wonderful things in life when we close our minds to the possibilities of the unimaginable," the Tree of Wisdom replied. And with that, it shook its branches lightly and covered the two children with a shower of leaves.

Tommy and Pia cried out with delight and raced around the tree's trunk. Soon, there were enough leaves gathered on the grass for them to have a leaf fight. They swooped up armfuls of green leaves and chased each other around until they were both out of breath.

When it was time for Tommy to go home, he gave Pia a hug with a smile and said, "Thank you for sharing the magic of the tree with me. I know now to give people a chance to prove their point before I brush them off."

STORY 3 – PIA AND THE MUD RACE

Pia was skipping alongside her father on their way to the village shops one evening when they came across Tommy and his mother all dressed up in trainers and running clothes.

"We are getting ready for a charity mud race in two weeks to raise money for a homeless shelter," Tommy's mother explained when Pia asked what they were doing. "Why don't you join us?"

Her father seemed quite interested in the idea and asked for more details, but Pia wasn't so sure.

She had never been very good at races. She loved to run out in the garden because there were no rules there to follow, but running in competitions always made her nervous. There were always kids with longer legs or better strength who piped her to the post.

But that wasn't even the main problem.

Pia did not like to get muddy. When the tiniest splatter of mud got on her shoes, she was always quick to wipe it off so that it wouldn't stick. On rainy days, she made sure to carefully step around puddles in the road. And she remembered to wipe down Dusty, who didn't mind jumping in puddles at all, before she let him back into the house.

"It's not about who comes first or last," Tommy assured her, when she voiced her concern to him later on. "It's about the money we can raise and donate for a good cause. It really is a lot of fun, we get to climb over great big foam rocks and crawl through muddy tunnels. There's even a massive mud slide right at the end."

Pia thought the donation part sounded great, but she really couldn't think of any way she would have fun if it meant having her entire body covered in mud. She nodded along and pretended not to mind when they got home and her father signed them all up.

When Pia took Dusty out for a walk in the garden, her face was twisted with worry.

"What troubles you, young girl?" the Tree of Wisdom asked as she came closer. Its branches reached down as if to comfort her.

Pia sighed and leaned on its trunk and watched Dusty as he raced around her feet. She told the tree her worries, even though she couldn't see what good it would do.

"Tell me this, what is the worst thing that could happen if you get muddy?" the tree enquired kindly.

Pia didn't need to think long to give an answer. "I'll get the house dirty when I go back in, and I'll have to change my clothes and take a bath even if it's only the middle of the day."

"And what's the worst thing that could happen if you don't help to raise money for the homeless shelter?"

Pia paused to think a little longer this time. She hadn't really considered things from that point of view. She had only been thinking of herself and her own fears. She didn't have an answer for the tree, so when she went back to the house, she went to her mother to ask her what the charity did.

"They help people who don't have anywhere to stay by giving them a warm bed for the night and some food to eat," her mother explained.

She showed Pia the website of the charity they would be helping. Pia was surprised to see so many children who needed somewhere to spend the night. Even though she still wasn't sure how to overcome her concerns, she could see that the money from the race would do others a lot of good.

She now had an answer for the Tree of Wisdom.

"If I take part in the mud race," she said to it when she went back outside, "my clothes and hair will get muddy for just one day, but there will be a child who will have a safe place to sleep and a hot meal to eat for many nights to come."

"You are correct. Even though we may suffer brief moments of discomfort whilst doing something good, we need to keep our focus on the end goal and not so much on our temporary struggles."

With the other kids in mind, Pia was now motivated to get ready for the race. Tommy offered to train with her, but his garden wasn't as big as Pia's, so he came over to practise with her the next day.

The children put on their trainers and went out to the back garden with Dusty. As they got closer to the tree, Pia noticed something very odd. Although it hadn't rained in days, the ground around the base of the Tree of Wisdom was completely covered in mud.

There were a few small mounds of earth clustered around in places, and big puddles where the damp earth had sunk in. Pia realised the tree had created an obstacle course for them.

"This is amazing!" Tommy gasped.

"How did you do all this?" Pia asked.

The tree shook its branches and a drizzle of water fell onto the ground.

"I soaked up all the water from the morning dew and let it fall all around me," it said. "When the ground was nicely damp, I pushed and pulled at my roots to form the mounds and the puddles."

Pia was truly amazed, but she was beginning to realise that the oak tree was so much more than just a talking tree.

"What are you waiting for?" it shook its branches again and soaked Tommy and Pia with water from head to foot. "This will help you get over your fear of being muddy."

At first, Pia was cautious and took a small step towards the water soaked patch of earth. But Dusty didn't share her worries, and he ran ahead and dived onto one of the mounds, splashing mud all around him. A big clump landed right on Pia's clean white shorts, and she took a deep breath.

Pia was about to cry out in alarm when she noticed that Tommy's clothes were also covered in mud. And he didn't seem bothered about it one tiny bit. Instead he grinned from ear to ear as he ran ahead to join Dusty in the mud.

They both looked like they were having so much fun climbing on top of the mounds and splashing around the muddy puddles that Pia forgot her concerns about messing up her clothes and ran forward to join her friends. She didn't even notice that her entire outfit was getting splattered as she ran.

The children squealed with laughter and played under the tree for a very long time. When it was time to go back to the house, they were both so completely covered in mud, it was almost impossible to tell which child was which.

The tree shook its leaves once again, and this time it helped wash away some of the mud from Pia and Tommy's faces. When they got back to the house, Pia became worried again, this time because she thought her mother would be upset at all the mess they had made.

"What happened here?" her mother laughed when she came outside and saw the two muddy children and dog. She grabbed the garden hose and sprayed them both down with water, but her smile never left her face.

"You're not cross?" Pia asked when they were both thoroughly soaking wet and clean.

"Not at all," her mother said. "I'm glad to see you are taking the race seriously. I wasn't sure if you would be able to get over your fear of mud, and now I see you've embraced it full on."

When the day of the race finally arrived, Pia had more fun than she could have imagined, and the two families helped raise a lot of money for the homeless shelter. Pia couldn't believe she had almost let her worrying stop her from doing something good for others.

"From now on, I am never going to limit myself from experiencing life and having fun, just because of my fears," Pia said to her mother as they all received their shiny medals for completing the race.

STORY 4 – PIA AND THE LOST BRACELET

"Do you remember all the ingredients we need to get?" Pia's father asked as they stood outside the busy grocery store in the village.

Pia nodded before listing out what she had memorised, counting off on her small fingers.

"Apples, rhubarb stalks, brown sugar, flour and butter."

"And don't forget the oats, to give that extra crumbly crunch," her father reminded her before they entered the store.

Pia was really excited because he had promised to show her how to make her mother's favourite dessert, apple and rhubarb crumble. Pia also loved the dessert, and she was already dreaming about how yummy it would taste as they walked through the store and picked out all the items on the list.

It didn't take long for them to pay for everything, and they were off home again.

As they walked past the village square, Pia noticed a small playground inside it with some brightly coloured equipment set up. There was a seesaw, a sandbox, a merry-go-round, a swing set, and a slide.

Even though she had been having a lot of fun with Dusty in the garden, Pia really wanted to play with all the things she remembered from the playground in the city.

"Please, can I go in there?" she asked her father eagerly.

He paused and glanced at his watch. "Only for a little while so that the butter doesn't melt," he said, sitting on a bench nearby, "and then we have to get back home to make dinner."

Pia raced into the playground. She wasn't sure where to start. She loved to swing and also loved the motion of the seesaw as she went up and down in the air. But there was no one else in the playground to join her except for one little girl who was wildly digging through the sandbox.

The girl didn't look like she wanted to be disturbed, but Pia decided to ask her anyway.

"Don't talk to me," the girl snapped, even before Pia could speak, "I don't have time for you."

Pia was surprised by her harsh words. What could possibly be so important in a sandbox that would make the girl so rude? But as she turned to walk away, Pia realised the girl's voice had been shaky when she spoke.

"Is everything alright?" she asked.

The girl sighed and stopped her digging.

"I'm sorry for being so crabby, but I can't find my silver charm bracelet," she said. "My godmother gave it to me when I went to visit her last year. It was around my wrist when I got here, but it must have fallen into the sand."

Pia could see why she was so upset. If she lost something so precious, she would feel the same way. Even though Pia would have preferred to ride the seesaw or fly high on the swing, she decided to help the girl as best as she could.

"If we both search for it, we might find it quicker," Pia offered, and to her relief, the girl agreed.

They dug through the sandbox, from right to left and then all the way back, but the bracelet didn't turn up. It didn't help matters that it was now getting dark. Pia had a feeling they wouldn't be able to find the small bracelet in all that sand.

"There's no point in carrying on," the girl said with a heavy sigh, "it is gone forever and I will have to tell my mum."

But Pia didn't want to give up so easily. Searching for a solution to the problem, she remembered how the Tree of Wisdom had helped her recently when she found herself in difficult situations. She wondered what the tree would say if it was there with them that moment.

Closing her eyes briefly, she imagined its voice in her head.

"When you have a problem, if you keep trying one thing and keep getting the same results, maybe it is time to look for another approach," the sound of the tree's rustling leaves drifted gently into her mind.

When Pia opened her eyes, she had on a bright smile.

"Do you believe in magic?" she asked the downcast girl.

The girl's eyes lit up for the first time.

"Of course!" she said with no hesitation. "My mother says magic is in here," she pointed to her chest, "and all around us."

"I also believe in magic, and it has allowed me to speak to my wise, old friend who has a suggestion," Pia said. "Now, you have to close your eyes and think of all the things you did when you came into the playground."

The girl closed her eyes and frowned as she went back in time in her head.

"First of all, I played on the swing set and rode around on the merry-go-round, but it was no fun doing this on my own. So I climbed up the ladder and whooshed down the slide before I came to the sandbox."

"And have you checked by the merry-go-round, or the swing set or the slide?" Pia asked.

When the girl nodded, Pia wasn't sure what else to do. It was beginning to feel like the bracelet might really be lost forever.

"Let's go look again," she suggested, trying not to lose hope. "Two sets of eyes are usually better than one, at least that's what my mum always says."

And so, they left the sandbox and went to look in all three places again. But the bracelet was still nowhere in sight.

By this time, the sun was going down, and Pia's father and the girl's mother had come into the playground area to take them both home.

"What's the matter?" her father asked when they met them still searching the ground with sad faces.

"She's lost her bracelet and we can't seem to find it anywhere."

"Oh no!" the girl's mother exclaimed. "That's your favourite bracelet from your godmother."

The little girl looked close to tears. "I have no idea where it fell off. We've looked everywhere I can possibly think of."

"Wait, do you mean that bracelet?" Pia's father asked, pointing high above their heads.

All their eyes followed the direction of his finger. And there, caught at the top of the ladder which led to the slide, was a shiny silver charm bracelet.

The little girl cried out with joy and ran up the ladder to bring down her bracelet.

"Thank you so much," the girl said with tears of relief. "We searched everywhere and I really thought I'd lost it."

"I'm glad I could help," Pia's father said. "When you can't find a solution to a problem, it is okay to ask others for help. They might be able to see things differently and help you find the answer you've been seeking."

"I will definitely remember that," the girl said before leaving the playground with her grateful mother.

Once they were gone, Pia's father extended his hand to her. "Are you ready to go home? Mum must be really hungry by now."

Pia smiled up at him and nodded, knowing her mother would be okay with their little delay when she found out they had spent the time helping a stranger.

STORY 5 – PIA AND THE TRAINING WHEELS

"Aunt Vera and your cousins, Angelica and Zara, will be visiting for a few days next week," Pia's mother announced one morning when she came down for breakfast.

Pia was very happy to hear this. She loved her aunt and cousins very dearly, and she hadn't seen them in such a long time. They had moved to another country for Aunt Vera's job. Since there were still a few weeks left before school started, having them around would make the summer break even more special.

On the day of their arrival, Pia was practically bursting with excitement. She helped her mother get the guestroom ready and put out fresh flowers in a vase. When they heard the toot of a car horn, she could barely contain herself.

"Aunt Vera!" Pia jumped into her aunt's arms when they met them outside, standing next to a shiny red smart car.

"Little Pia, you've grown so big," her aunt observed, and Pia beamed from ear to ear.

Her Aunt Vera looked exactly the same as Pia remembered, with her large red framed glasses and dyed bright red hair. On the other hand, Pia's cousins had both grown a lot since the last time she had seen them two years ago.

At twelve years old, Angelica was very tall and had on big yellow sunglasses which looked like they covered half of her face. She held a mobile phone and only looked up once from the screen to greet Pia's mother. All she managed to give Pia was a grunt before her gaze went back to her phone.

Zara had been a wobbly toddler who always clung onto a pink blanket, but now she was walking about very confidently. Unlike Angelica, she seemed quite pleased to see Pia and her mother, and she hugged them very tightly.

"Preteen drama," Aunt Vera tried to explain Angelica's odd behaviour, but Pia didn't know what that meant. She just thought it was very rude of Angelica to pretend they weren't even there.

When they had settled in and had some food to eat, Pia decided it was time for her cousins to meet the tree. She was sure Angelica would be interested in meeting a tree who could talk and do so many wonderful things.

But Angelica didn't even look up when Pia tried to get her to come into the garden. Instead, she continued to tap away on her phone, swiping the screen as she watched videos and played games. There was no way she was going to meet the tree like that.

"Why is Angelica always on that phone?" Pia asked Zara on their way to visit the tree.

"Mummy said that's where she talks to her friends from school," Zara replied with a pout. "But I wish she would stop to teach me how to ride my bicycle as she promised at the start of summer."

Pia thought it was a shame Angelica wasn't spending more time with Zara. She wished she had a sister to play with all the time. Although she had Tommy and Dusty to keep her company, she knew she would always make sure Zara had a smile on her face if she lived with her.

She suddenly had an idea. "I could teach you how to ride on my bicycle. We still have the training wheels I used years ago, and it wasn't too difficult to learn."

"Thank you so much," Zara hugged her cousin, "I can't wait to start."

"What's all the excitement about?" the Tree of Wisdom asked when they arrived at its base. "And who is this pretty young lady with you today?"

Zara's mouth hung open in surprise.

"This is my cousin, Zara. She's visiting and I'm going to teach her how to ride my bicycle, just like my mum taught me," Pia smiled with pride.

"That's a very useful skill to learn, but you have to remember to wear a helmet to protect yourself if you fall," the tree advised.

Zara recovered enough to speak. "You can really talk."

"I can do more than talk," the tree replied.

And right before their eyes, the ground around the tree began to harden, and all the grass sank into the earth, leaving a perfectly firm ring around its trunk.

"Whenever you want to ride your bicycle, you can do so under my shade. It's much too hot in the sun this week."

The girls clapped with joy and ran back to the house to ask Pia's father to help put the old training wheels on her bicycle.

"Angelica will help you out," Aunt Vera insisted when she heard of their plan. "Since she's older, she can make sure you're both safe."

Pia was glad her aunt was getting her older cousin involved. But Angelica didn't like this new plan at all.

"I don't want to spend all day with them," she protested, "I don't have time for kiddie stuff. There's so much to catch up with on my phone with my friends."

But her mother wouldn't hear of it, and the next day, a grumpy Angelica was forced into the garden with the girls and the bicycle. She took so long to come out that Pia and Zara went to the tree first to have a chat.

"I can't understand why Angelica is always on her phone," Pia repeated. "She's missing out on meeting you, and playing with Dusty and Zara and me."

"Do you remember when I told you that not everyone older is wiser?" the tree asked. "She's lost in her own world and wasting a perfect summer's day, but I'm sure your cousin will come to appreciate the things around her when it matters the most."

"We are here by the tree," Zara called out to Angelica when she finally made it out of the house.

"That's ridiculous, you can't learn to ride a bicycle on grass," Angelica yelled back at them. "The best place to be is here on the back porch."

Pia frowned. "Are you sure about that? There's a loose tile over there that Daddy has been meaning to fix."

Angelica had already gone back to looking at her phone. The only advantage of staying on the porch was that she could sit on one of the deckchairs under the shade. With sad sighs, Pia and Zara bid the tree goodbye and went back to the porch.

Pia helped Zara onto the bicycle, and then began to guide her around, just like her mother had done for her a few years ago. Zara turned out to be a quick learner, and soon she was pedalling confidently, with the training wheels helping her along.

It was all going so well, until Zara got a little too keen and shot off with the bicycle. Before Pia could stop her, she was heading straight for the corner of the porch with the loose tile.

"No, Zara, stop!" Pia cried.

Zara pressed down on the brakes, trying to stop, but one of the training wheels got caught on the tile, and she went crashing down. At that very moment, a strong gust of wind blew some leaves over from the garden. With the leaves as a bed, the wind lifted Zara up into the air before she could hurt herself too badly, and then lowered her gently onto the ground.

"Are you alright?" Angelica jumped up in a panic and ran to her little sister.

Zara nodded, and showed them a small graze on her arm. "I only scrapped my hand a little."

"I'm so sorry I wasn't paying attention," Angelica sounded like she meant it as she kissed Zara's cheek. "You could have been badly hurt and I was just watching a silly video. I should have listened when Pia said there was a loose tile here. I promise I'll focus now and keep you safe."

As the girls went into the house to tend to Zara's wound, Angelica stopped Pia by the door.

"Did you see the leaves rise up, or was that my imagination?" Angelica whispered to her cousin with an uncertain tone.

Pia just smiled and said, "I'll show you how that happened in a little while."

Later, Pia and Zara went back to the tree with a very confused Angelica behind them. She wasn't sure whether Angelica would be willing to free her senses to hear it speak. It didn't seem like she wanted to be involved with anything that wasn't on her phone.

"Thank you for saving me," Zara ran up to the Tree of Wisdom and gave it a hug.

"You're welcome," the tree replied, sprinkling some leaves on her head and making her giggle. "I had some help from my windy friend. You should thank her next time she blows this way. Now, do you want to keep practising out here where it's safe?"

As the tree spoke, the ground around its base hardened in a ring shape like it had done before.

It was Angelica's turn to be stunned into silence as she stared on in wonder. And with something as unimaginable as a talking magical tree right there in the back garden, that was the last time she spent all day staring at her phone for the rest of their stay at Heely.

STORY 6 – PIA AND THE BOY WHO SAID TOO LITTLE

It was finally the first day of school and Pia could hardly breathe with the excitement she felt. Her mother had just dropped her off at her new school, which was around the corner from the village square.

There were so many new faces in her class and Pia was nervous to approach anyone, but Tommy was there to help put her at ease. At break time, she met all of his friends, and they all went to play outside in the sun.

"Who is that sitting by himself in the corner?" Pia asked after she noticed a boy all on his own.

"Oh, that's just Weird Billy," Tommy explained. "He barely says a word all day, which makes him really odd."

Billy looked so miserable sitting alone and drawing in a blue notebook, Pia decided to go say hello. But Tommy quickly held her back as he looked around to make sure no one had noticed.

"If you talk to him, everyone will think you're odd too."

Although Pia couldn't see what the harm was, she left the boy alone. Tommy had been there longer than she had, and he had to know what he was talking about. She spent the rest of break time playing with Tommy and his friends instead.

But every day, Pia would glance at the quiet boy in the corner and wonder what he was thinking as he scribbled in his notebook. He always looked up at the other kids with sadness in his eyes, and Pia knew he really wanted to join in on their fun. There had to be a reason he was so very quiet.

"True courage is the ability to reach out to people even when nobody else wants to," the tree said to her when she mentioned the boy one evening after school.

"What if nobody talks to me after?" Pia asked, still a little concerned about Tommy's words.

The Tree of Wisdom replied gently, "We must remember that if we are doing the right thing, it is not always important what others think of us. Your true friends will never abandon you."

The next week, Pia's teacher, Mrs Herbert, announced that the class would be going to the school's allotment the next day to help plant autumn vegetables, and the pupils would work in twos. Pia saw her chance and quietly asked Mrs Herbert to pair her up with Billy.

When they got to the allotment, Pia smiled warmly at Billy.

"Hi, I'm Pia," she said and knelt beside him.

The boy nodded at her and kept his head down, starting to dig the soil with the little trowel they had been given.

Pia frowned. There had to be a way to get him to speak to her.

"What's in that notebook you write in?" she asked.

When he didn't answer, she continued to question him. "Is it something secret?"

She followed that up with a few more questions. Eventually, the boy realised Pia would keep going if he didn't say something. He opened his mouth to speak, and then shut it again. He seemed to be considering if he should make the effort to respond.

"I-it i-is a di-a-ary," he said eventually.

Pia realised what the problem was. Billy had a stutter and he was shy about it. That was probably why he never said anything to the other kids. She knew this because her friend, Carissa, back in the city had also had a stutter and had been incredibly nervous about it.

"I would like to keep a diary one day," Pia carried on, like she hadn't noticed.

When she didn't laugh at him or make any other comment, the boy braved another reply.

"I-it i-is w-wri-tten in c-co-de," he continued.

Pia nodded. "That's very clever, so nobody can read it except for you. When I start my own diary, I'll also write it in code."

In the end, they spent the whole time chatting as they dug up the earth, ready for Mrs Herbert to show them how to plant their seeds. Billy seemed very happy. Even though it took him a while to get the words out, Pia waited patiently and responded in no hurry.

"What were you doing with Weird Billy?" Tommy asked Pia at break time.

"There's nothing wrong with Billy," she said. "He's really nice, and I'm not going to ignore him or call him weird because everyone else does. Did you know he also has a log fort to spot otters, just like you do?"

"I had no idea," Tommy admitted.

"Well, if you never give him a chance, you'll never get to know all the other wonderful things about him. Why don't we go over to him now and say hello? But you have to remember to give him a moment to speak."

Tommy was worried the other kids would call him odd, but he really wanted to hear more about Billy's otter spotting fort. He didn't know anyone else who had one just like he did. So, he followed Pia and she introduced the two boys. In no time at all, they realised they had a lot more in common and chatted all through break time.

After school, Mrs Herbert took Pia to the side. "I would like to thank you for what you did for Billy. He is really shy and needs friends like you."

Pia was really glad she had listened to the Tree of Wisdom and had the courage to stand up for Billy. In the end, she hadn't just made a friend, she had also given him the gift of friendship with others.

STORY 7 – PIA AND THE BIG CHANGE

A cool breeze blew through Pia's back garden. Even though she didn't mind it too much, it was close to the end of September and her mother had started to insist she should wear a jumper whenever she went outside.

That day, Pia was watering the small herb garden she and her mother had planted a few weeks ago. It was then she noticed some of the leaves on the Tree of Wisdom were no longer their usual dark shade of green. Instead, there were a few shades of yellow-orange and reddish brown leaves mixed in.

Pia went closer to get a better view of what was happening to her beloved tree.

"You seem worried, young girl," the tree said when Pia continued to stare up at its different coloured leaves.

"Are you unwell?" she asked quietly. "Your leaves are changing colour."

Over the years, Pia had seen this happen to some other trees in the city when the weather turned cold, but she had never thought to ask why.

The tree chuckled lightly. "Not at all. This is simply the cycle I must follow," it explained. "Every living thing has to let life take its course, even big, old oak trees like me."

"But when my mother's potted plants have their leaves turn brown, they usually don't last much longer," Pia's concerns remained.

The tree's voice was gentle as it spoke. "That might be true for some plants, but the only way I can live on is if my leaves dry up and fall away so that I can use all of my energy to brace myself for the coming winter weather."

Pia considered this for a moment. "If all your leaves will be gone for the winter months, doesn't this mean you won't be your full self?"

"Yes," the tree confirmed, "with my leaves gone, I will need to keep quiet so that I can stand strong."

Pia gasped at this. "What will I do without you then?"

"Young girl, sometimes in life, we have to be patient and learn to sacrifice some things we cherish in order to achieve what will make us better and tougher."

Pia wasn't thrilled with this news, but she trusted that the wise tree's words were true. Besides, she had no choice in the matter. Even though she willed the leaves to stay green, they just kept turning redder and yellower as the days went by.

By the middle of October, most of the leaves had turned brown and started to fall off the Tree of Wisdom. And as this happened, the tree said less and less with each passing day.

Although the tree had explained all this to her, it still made Pia sad as it grew quieter throughout the winter months. At one point, right in the dead of winter, the tree stood completely silent. Not much could be heard out in the garden except for the howling of the north wind and the traffic noise from the busy road on the other side of the hedge.

Pia was sure the tree must have been incredibly lonely as it stood out there completely bare in the cold, with no bushytailed grey squirrels to run up and down its trunk, and not a single leaf to catch the freezing rain and snow which fell on its branches.

And even though Pia wanted to visit the tree as often as before, it was much too cold to stand outside. She only went out for short walks in the garden with Dusty and had to be covered in layers of warm jumpers and scarves. So she listened to the tree's advice and waited patiently for the warmth of the sun to return.

One day in early March, Pia noticed some green leaves sprouting from the damp earth at the bottom of the tree.

"Springtime is nearly here," her mother confirmed when Pia told her about the shoots. "The daffodils will bloom soon and everything that was asleep will start to come back to life."

This filled Pia with hope and she went out each day to check on her friend. But even though the ground around the tree was quickly covered in beautiful yellow daffodils and purple crocuses, the Tree of Wisdom remained bare and silent.

It wasn't until mid-April when the sun was out in the sky for longer hours and the birds woke up early to sing each morning that the first signs of leaves began to appear on the old oak tree. By then, Pia had learnt not to get overexcited by the changes. She waited patiently until the leaves had grown bigger before she approached the tree.

"Don't stand so far away," the tree's words came out in a faint whisper, almost like it was still trying to find its voice.

Pia was so pleased to hear it speak, she rushed forward and hugged the tree's trunk.

"I'm so glad you're back," she cried with relief. "I was so worried when the daffodils came out and you weren't here."

"You must understand that every living thing has a different path to take," the tree said calmly. "Everything needs a certain time to develop in their own natural way, including you, young girl."

"But why did it take so long for you to return?" Pia asked.

"Although the smaller plants were able to come out much earlier, I am much bigger and had to stay quiet until my strength was properly restored.

And now that the weather is warm enough, my leaves can return in full force in an even deeper green shade than they were before."

"I have so much to tell you," Pia said, remembering all that had happened over the last few months. "I tried to speak to you sometimes, but it wasn't very easy with the cold."

"I knew you were keeping watch over me," the tree assured her. "I was grateful for your company every time you came out here, even though I couldn't say the words to you. Now I can finally show you exactly how I feel."

To Pia's amazement, the tree lowered a branch and lifted her onto it. She gently touched its new leaves which were still very small and light green, and then she held on tightly as the Tree of Wisdom carefully moved her from one branch to another as it raised her high up into the air. When it finally stopped, she was so high up that she could see far into the distance for what looked like miles and miles.

To the right, she saw Tommy's house which stood close to the river and provided him with a good hiding place to watch the otters. And to the left she spotted the village square with the playground where all the children gathered to play. She could even see her new school tucked away on the other side of the square.

"This is the best view I've ever had!" Pia declared.

"Something special for a very special friend," the tree's voice rang out with a smile. "Thank you for waiting patiently for my return."

Over the next few months, Pia saw for herself what a great difference the tree's period of solitude and silence had made. Stronger than ever, the Tree of Wisdom bloomed with flowers, and small acorns began to appear not long after. By the start of summer, the tree was even more magnificent than Pia remembered.

With this experience, she learnt to let go and let life's natural changes take place because everything worked out alright in the end for the mighty, old and wise oak tree with a little patience and a lot of self-belief.

DISCLAIMER

This book contains opinions and ideas of the author and is meant to teach the reader informative and helpful knowledge while due care should be taken by the user in the application of the information provided. The instructions and strategies are possibly not right for every reader and there is no guarantee that they work for everyone. Using this book and implementing the information/recipes therein contained is explicitly your own responsibility and risk. This work with all its contents, does not guarantee correctness, completion, quality or correctness of the provided information. Misinformation or misprints cannot be completely eliminated.

Printed in Great Britain
by Amazon